To:
FROM GRAMMA BETZ
XMAS 2021

DID DINOSAURS LAY EGGS?

First published in the USA 1997 by
Benchmark Books
Marshall Cavendish Corporation
99 White Plains Road
Tarrytown, New York 10591-9001

Devised and produced by Tucker Slingsby Ltd,
London House, 66-68 Upper Richmond Road,
London SW15 2RP

Copyright © Tucker Slingsby Ltd, 1997

All rights reserved. Without limiting the rights under copyright reserved above,
no part of this publication may be reproduced, stored in or introduced into a retrieval
system, or transmitted, in any form or by any means (electronic, mechanical, photocopying,
recording or otherwise), without the prior written permission of both the copyright owner
and the above publisher of this book.

Designed by Helen James
Color separations by Positive Colour, Maldon, Essex, Great Britain
Printed and bound in Italy

ISBN 0-7614-0497-X

Library of Congress Cataloging-in-Publication Data

Parker, Steve.
   Did dinosaurs lay eggs? / Steve Parker ; illustrated by Graham
Rosewarne.
      p.   cm. -- (Ask about animals)
  Includes index.
  Summary: Describes different types of dinosaurs and reconstructs
their habitats and behavior.
  ISBN 0-7614-0497-X (lib. bdg.)
  1. Dinosaurs--Juvenile literature. [1. Dinosaurs.]
I. Rosewarne, Graham, ill. II. Title. III. Series: Parker, Steve.
Ask about animals.
QE862.D5P1456 1997
567.9'1--dc20   96-13378
                                                                   CIP
                                                                   AC

DID DINOSAURS LAY EGGS?

Steve Parker

Illustrated by Graham Rosewarne

BENCHMARK BOOKS

MARSHALL CAVENDISH
NEW YORK

Introduction

How long did dinosaurs live on the Earth? The Age of the Dinosaurs lasted for about 160 million years. That is a long time considering humans have only existed for three million years.

The first dinosaurs appeared on the Earth about 230 million years ago. Their world was very different from the world today. We know about this and about dinosaurs themselves mainly from their fossils. These are bones, teeth, claws, and other remains preserved in rocks. Fossils tell us that dinosaurs were types of animals called reptiles. Some were big, others were small. Some ate plants, others ate meat. Some even ate the eggs that other female dinosaurs laid.

Our knowledge of dinosaurs is the result of years of careful work by experts all over the world. It's a huge detective story, with fossils as the clues. But we can never be absolutely sure what dinosaurs were like, because no one has ever seen a living dinosaur.

Contents

Did dinosaurs...

Leave us clues?	6
Lay eggs?	8
Live in groups?	10
Talk to each other?	12
Eat grass?	14
Eat each other?	16
Have scaly skins?	18
Tower over trees?	20
Use weapons?	22
Run quickly?	24
Go swimming?	26
Have wings?	28
Why did dinosaurs die out?	30
Will dinosaurs ever return?	32
Index	32

DID DINOSAURS...
Leave us clues?

They did. But not on purpose, of course. As dinosaurs lived and died, they left behind parts of their bodies and signs of their lives. Soft body parts, such as the flesh, soon rotted away. Harder parts, such as bones, teeth, claws, horns, skin, and eggs, lasted longer. Some of these have been preserved in the rocks for millions of years and have turned to stone. We call them fossils. Experts find and dig up these fossils. They use them as clues to work out how dinosaurs looked, lived, were born, got old, and died.

Fossil bones can tell us a lot about an animal. Skull bones from inside the head provide good clues. The holes in the skull show the size and shape of the dinosaur's brain, eyes, ears, and mouth. This long, narrow fossil skull was dug out of the desert. It has a very large brain case so the dinosaur it belonged to, **Dromiceiomimus** (dro-miss-ee-oh-my-mus), must have been brainy!

Animal teeth are very hard and tough. In fact, they are usually the hardest parts of the body so they often get preserved as fossils. This is lucky, because the shape of the teeth gives clues to what the animal ate. **Heterodontosaurus** (het-er-oh-dont-oh-saw-rus) had teeth of different shapes, which was unusual for a dinosaur. This means it probably ate lots of different foods.

DID DINOSAURS LEAVE US CLUES?

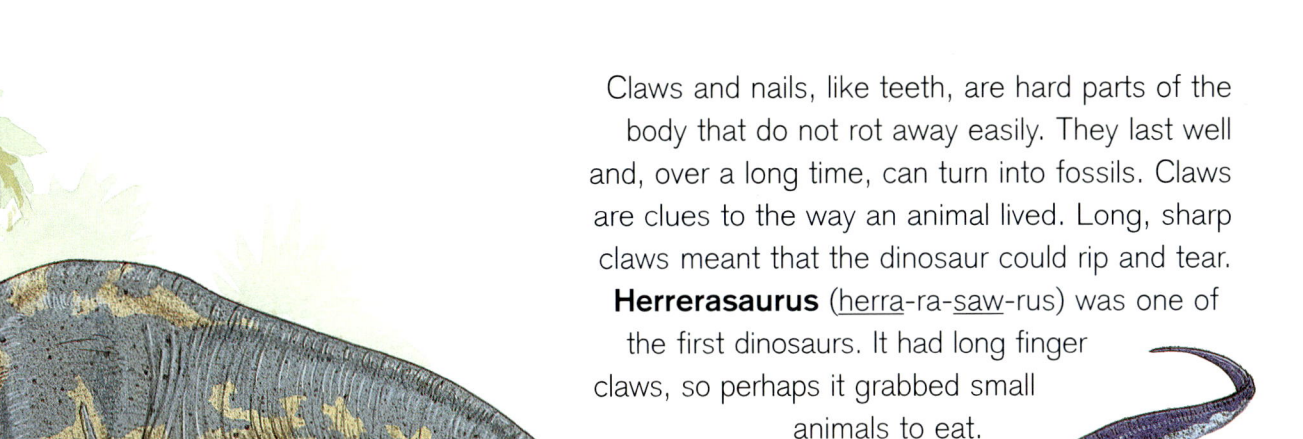

Claws and nails, like teeth, are hard parts of the body that do not rot away easily. They last well and, over a long time, can turn into fossils. Claws are clues to the way an animal lived. Long, sharp claws meant that the dinosaur could rip and tear. **Herrerasaurus** (herra-ra-saw-rus) was one of the first dinosaurs. It had long finger claws, so perhaps it grabbed small animals to eat.

Dinosaurs left behind other things that have become fossils, too. Sometimes their droppings went dry and hard, became covered by dust or mud, and were preserved. Huge dinosaurs, such as **Riojasaurus**, (ree-ok-a-saw-rus) left huge piles of dino-dung. The bits and pieces in the droppings, such as pieces of twigs and seeds, are clues to what the dinosaur ate. Luckily, after millions of years, the dung has turned to stone so it doesn't smell!

Even footprints can become clues! When dinosaurs walked on sand or mud, the prints they left sometimes became hard and fossilized. This is how we know that dinosaurs such as **Camarasaurus** (kam-ar-a-saw-rus) lived in groups. The dinosaurs left many tracks as the herd walked along together.

7

DID DINOSAURS...
Lay eggs?

Yes, they did. Dinosaurs belonged to a group of animals called reptiles. Reptiles alive today include crocodiles, lizards, turtles, and snakes. Most female reptiles lay eggs which hatch into babies. As dinosaurs were reptiles, they laid eggs too. Experts have dug up fossil eggs buried millions of years ago. They have even found the fossil remains of a dinosaur called Oviraptor sitting on its nest and eggs.

Fossil hunters first found fossil dinosaur eggs in 1922, in the Gobi Desert in Mongolia. The eggs were laid millions of years ago by **Protoceratops** (pro-toh-serra-tops), a dinosaur about the size of a pig. The female Protoceratops scraped a hole in the sand. Then she laid about 30 potato-sized eggs, arranging them neatly in a spiral.

Maiasaura (my-a-saw-ra) was as long as a double-decker bus. It had a wide, flat mouth, like the bill of a duck, and no front teeth. Huge groups of these dinosaurs made nests in the ground, covering entire hillsides. The females laid eggs in hollows scooped out of the earth or mud. They may also have brought food to the nest for their babies to eat.

DID DINOSAURS LAY EGGS?

Some dinosaurs may have protected their eggs and their newly hatched young. **Styracosaurus** (sty-rak-oh-saw-rus) was a large dinosaur, bigger than a car, with long, sharp horns on its head. Few other animals would have tried to attack and eat it. But if a hungry, hunting dinosaur came near, the young dinosaurs could have been at risk. To protect them, the adults might have formed a circle, facing outwards with their horns towards the attacker. The young dinosaurs would have stayed in the center, safe from danger.

Eggs are a good food. Many animals today, such as snakes and mongooses (and people), eat them. Some dinosaurs probably ate the eggs of other dinosaurs. **Oviraptor** (ohv-ih-rap-tor) was a speedy, dog-sized dinosaur with long, strong fingers. It lived at the same time and in the same place as Protoceratops. It might have stolen eggs from Protoceratops' nests.

9

DID DINOSAURS...
Live in groups?

Yes, some dinosaurs probably lived with others of their kind, in a herd or pack. We know this from several clues. Some fossil footprints show that lots of the same kind of dinosaurs walked along the same route at the same time. They formed a herd that moved together. There are also fossil nests showing that dinosaurs of the same kind laid eggs near each other. They lived in a herd that bred together. Sometimes fossil bones are found in huge piles. This could mean hundreds of dinosaurs were preserved in the same place. They were a herd that died together.

Small dinosaurs such as **Lesothosaurus** (le-soo-too-saw-rus) would have been at the mercy of large predators. But these dog-sized, fast-running plant-eaters may have lived in a group. Each one would watch, listen, and sniff for danger. If one saw an enemy, it could have warned the others so they could escape.

Meat-eating **Indosuchus** (in-doh-soo-kus) probably did not live in a group. It would have crept up stealthily on plant-eating dinosaurs – one of them would have made a tasty meal. If there were lots of Indosuchus, the plant-eaters might have seen them and run away. A single hunter has more chance of catching its prey by surprise.

DID DINOSAURS LIVE IN GROUPS?

Small meat-eating dinosaurs could only have caught small prey. But if the dinosaurs had banded together into a group, they could have hunted much larger animals. This would have provided more meat for them to eat. Several **Ornitholestes** (or-<u>nith</u>-oh-<u>less</u>-teez) might have been able to kill a huge dinosaur by attacking it from all sides. The main benefit of hunting together is the killing power of the pack.

Iguanodon
(ig-<u>wa</u>-no-don) is one of the most famous dinosaurs. The fossilized bones of hundreds of these dinosaurs were found together in jumbled heaps. Perhaps they lived in a large herd for protection. Few predators attack a big group of animals. There is safety in numbers.

DID DINOSAURS...
Talk to each other?

Not exactly. They didn't speak using words, as we do, but many animals today send messages to others of their kind. Some "sing", making sounds such as hisses, squeaks, and roars. Others "dance", moving about in certain ways. They may also "wave flags", showing off brightly colored parts of their bodies. Other animals understand the messages. They could say "Danger! An enemy is nearby". Or "Stay away from my territory, the land where I live and feed". Or even "Would you like to mate with me?"

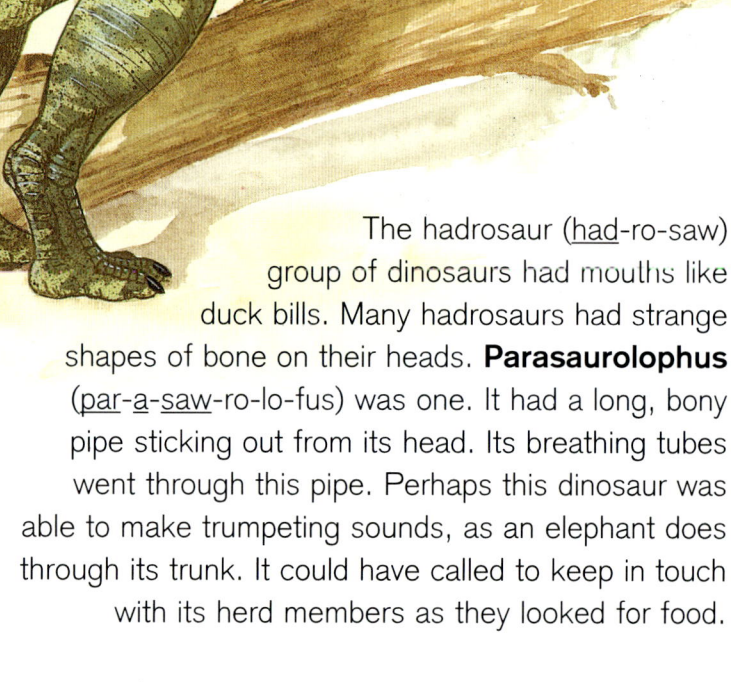

The hadrosaur (had-ro-saw) group of dinosaurs had mouths like duck bills. Many hadrosaurs had strange shapes of bone on their heads. **Parasaurolophus** (par-a-saw-ro-lo-fus) was one. It had a long, bony pipe sticking out from its head. Its breathing tubes went through this pipe. Perhaps this dinosaur was able to make trumpeting sounds, as an elephant does through its trunk. It could have called to keep in touch with its herd members as they looked for food.

Chasmosaurus (kaz-mo-saw-rus) belonged to a group called the ceratopsians (serra-top-see-ans), or "horn faces". It had huge frilly-edged flaps of skin on its neck. Imagine if these were brightly colored. The dinosaur could shake its head to send signals to other Chasmosaurus, or even to frighten off enemies.

DID DINOSAURS TALK TO EACH OTHER?

Corythosaurus (co-rith-oh-saw-rus) was another type of hadrosaur. It had a large, curved plate of bone sticking up from its head. This bony plate was hollow. Perhaps Corythosaurus blew its breathing air through the plate and made a sound like a car horn.

Edmontosaurus (ed-mont-oh-saw-rus) was also a hadrosaur. Marks on its nose bone show that it probably had a flap of skin there. Perhaps it could inflate the skin like a balloon to give a color and sound signal.

Psittacosaurus (si-tak-oh-saw-rus) was a ceratopsian, a relative of Chasmosaurus (opposite). Psittacosaurus means "parrot reptile". It had a very deep, beak-like mouth, just like a parrot or puffin. Perhaps others in its group identified it by the bright stripes on the beak.

As the old saying goes, actions speak louder than words.
Pachycephalosaurus (pak-ee-sef-al-lo-saw-rus) may have given its message by charging at its enemies and rivals. This dinosaur was unlikely to get hurt. It had a thick layer of bone on top of its head for protection.

DID DINOSAURS...
Eat grass?

Animals that eat plants are called herbivores. They usually have broad, flat teeth to chew their food well. The shape of some dinosaurs' fossil teeth and jaws suggest that they were herbivores. A few fossil dinosaurs even have the fossilized remains of their last meals in their bodies. But dinosaurs did not eat grass. How do we know? Because no fossil grasses have been found from the Age of Dinosaurs. Grass did not grow until long after dinosaurs died out.

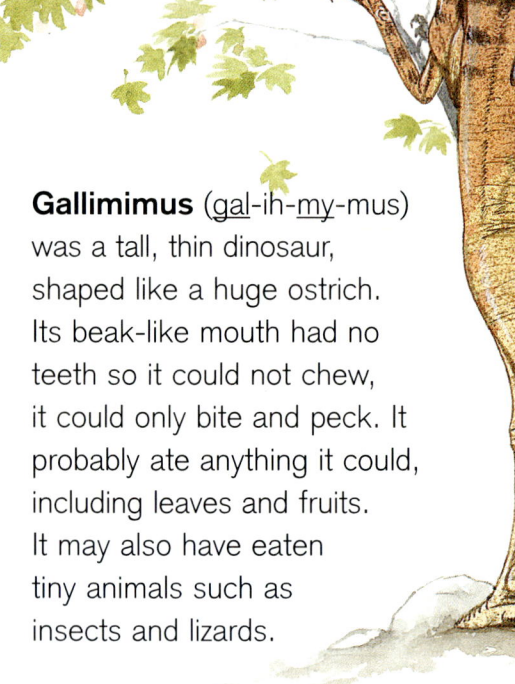

Gallimimus (gal-ih-my-mus) was a tall, thin dinosaur, shaped like a huge ostrich. Its beak-like mouth had no teeth so it could not chew, it could only bite and peck. It probably ate anything it could, including leaves and fruits. It may also have eaten tiny animals such as insects and lizards.

Plateosaurus (plat-ee-oh-saw-rus) was one of the first really large dinosaurs. Its teeth were like small blades, ideal for biting off and slicing up leaves. But it could not chew. This dinosaur might have reared up on its back legs to feed high in trees.

DID DINOSAURS EAT GRASS?

The duck-billed dinosaur **Kritosaurus** (cry-toh-saw-rus) had hundreds of teeth near the back of its mouth. They were broad and quite flat, but with sharp edges and ridges. Kritosaurus could probably chew up almost anything, even hard roots and woody stems.

Mamenchisaurus (ma-men-chee-saw-rus) had an extremely long neck. But its head was tiny and it had lots of strong, small teeth. This dinosaur could have swung its head around, and bitten and raked the leaves off trees. But it could not chew them. So Mamenchisaurus also ate stones! It swallowed them, and in its stomach these stones worked like a grinding mill to mash up its leafy food.

DID DINOSAURS...
Eat each other?

Yes, almost certainly. Animals that hunt and eat other animals are called carnivores. They have long, sharp teeth. Some dinosaurs also had sharp, pointed teeth. They were probably carnivores, too. Like carnivores today, these meat-eating dinosaurs had different ways of hunting. Some chased their prey. Others hid, waiting to leap out on their victims. Some hunted alone. Others formed packs. Scavenging dinosaurs fed on the leftover scraps of dead animals.

Wolves hunt in packs. They can attack a large animal such as a caribou or elk. During the Age of Dinosaurs, **Velociraptor** (vel-o-si-rap-tor) may have done the same. Several may have formed a group to hunt a large dinosaur. They could bite with their sharp teeth and slash with their claws. Their prey had little defense against an attack like this.

16

DID DINOSAURS EAT EACH OTHER?

Tarbosaurus (<u>tar</u>-bo-<u>saw</u>-rus), a huge meat-eater, was almost as tall as a house. It may have caught its prey by sprinting after it for a short time. Or perhaps Tarbosaurus arrived at a dead dinosaur killed by other animals, frightened the killers away, then ate its meal. Its teeth were bigger than your hands, and sharp enough to slice up flesh.

Dilophosaurus (dy-<u>lo</u>-fo-saw-rus) had long, thin, dagger-like teeth. They were ideal for jabbing at prey to kill it and for ripping off lumps of meat. Dilophosaurus also had long, slim legs. It may have been able to run twice as fast as you!

Some dinosaurs may have hunted mainly one kind of animal. **Baryonyx** (<u>bar</u>-ee-<u>on</u>-ix) had strong back legs for running, and a large thumb claw. Perhaps it waded through rivers and jabbed fish with its big claw, hooking them out of the water. Its mouth was like a crocodile's, long and narrow, and filled with small, sharp teeth. These teeth were suited to eating fish.

DID DINOSAURS...
Have scaly skins?

Yes. Fossils of scaly skin have been found with dinosaur bones, teeth, and other remains. The scales were hard enough to be preserved and turned to stone. Also, dinosaurs were reptiles. The reptiles alive today, such as lizards, snakes, and crocodiles, all have scaly skin. Scales are made of a tough, strong material called keratin. A dinosaur's scales protected its body. They also gave the dinosaur's skin its colors and patterns.

Elephant-sized **Stegosaurus** (steg-oh-saw-rus) had scaly skin. It also had huge, flat plates of bone sticking up along its back. It may have had bony shields on its hips, too. These plates of bone helped to protect the dinosaur from attack by meat-eaters. They may also have helped Stegosaurus to control its body temperature, so it did not get too warm or too cold.

Saltasaurus (salt-a-saw-rus) was a huge dinosaur. It had the usual small scales in its skin, but it also had two extra kinds of protection. Small, pea-sized lumps of bone were packed into the skin along the back and sides of Saltasaurus. Larger, higher lumps of bone, as big as your hand, were found on the dinosaur's back.

DID DINOSAURS HAVE SCALY SKINS?

Carnotaurus (carn-oh-<u>taw</u>-rus) was a meat-eating dinosaur. Pieces of its fossilized skin, showing thousands of scales, have been found. The scales were the size and shape of coins. Carnotaurus also had a strange, pointed, bony horn above each eye.

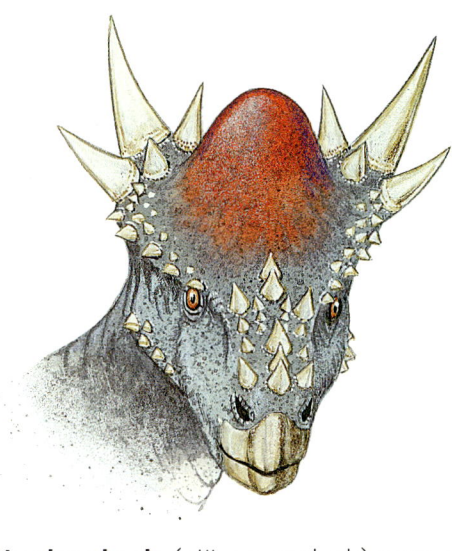

Stygimoloch (<u>stij</u>-ee-<u>mol</u>-ok) was a "bone-head" dinosaur. It had a thick plate of bone on top of its head, with rows of horns around it. This could have been for protection. Or perhaps it butted its rivals or enemies, as goats do today.

Spinosaurus (<u>spy</u>-no-<u>saw</u>-rus) had an unusual "sail" on its back. It was a flap of scaly skin held up by rods of bone that stuck up from its main backbone. The sail of Spinosaurus may have helped it to control its body temperature by picking up warm sun rays to heat its blood.

DID DINOSAURS...
Tower over trees?

Yes, some of them did. The largest dinosaurs were the sauropods. They had a huge barrel-shaped body, stumpy legs, a long whip-like tail, and a long neck with a tiny head. If they reared up and stretched their head and neck, they could reach more than 65 feet (20 meters) into the air. They would have towered over many trees.

Seismosaurus (size-mo-saw-rus) may have been the longest dinosaur. An adult was over 130 feet (40 meters) from nose to tail-tip, about as long as 10 family cars in a line. Seismosaurus probably swung its head, at the end of its long neck, to reach leaves high in the trees. Or perhaps to feed on plants on the ground.

Not all dinosaurs were giants. Tiny **Saltopus** (salt-oh-pus) was about the size of a chicken. Being small can be a good thing. Saltopus could have easily hidden from its enemies, among rocks, in a cave or in the under-growth. Also, it would not have needed to eat lots of food, as huge dinosaurs did.

DID DINOSAURS TOWER OVER TREES?

Torosaurus (tor-oh-saw-rus) could not tower over trees, but it had the biggest head of any dinosaur. In fact, the biggest head of any land animal that ever lived. The huge skull bones, and the large "flap" or frill over its neck, were over 7 feet (2.4 meters) long. That's the size of a large dining table!

Microceratops (my-cro-serra-tops) was a tiny dinosaur, about as long as a pet cat. It probably ran quickly on its two back legs. It belonged to the ceratopsian or "horn face" dinosaur group, so it was a close relative of huge Torosaurus (left).

The famous **Tyrannosaurus rex** (ty-ran-oh-saw-rus reks) was one of the biggest of all meat-eating dinosaurs. It was so tall, about 20 feet (6 meters) high when standing upright, that it could tower over a small tree. But it probably ran in a head-down position. Its huge head and sharp teeth then balanced the heavy tail over its back legs.

21

DID DINOSAURS...
Use weapons?

Yes, they certainly did! They did not have guns or bombs, of course. But dinosaurs did have swords, spears, daggers, whips, and clubs, and these could be very dangerous. A dinosaur's weapons were parts of its body – its tail, teeth, horns, or claws. The meat-eating dinosaurs used their weapons to catch, kill, and cut up their prey. The plant-eating dinosaurs had weapons to defend themselves and fight back against the meat-eaters. They may also have used their weapons to battle against rivals for control of their herd, or to win mates at breeding time.

If **Pentaceratops** (pen-ta-serra-tops) lowered its head and charged, you would soon get out of the way. This dinosaur's name means "five-horned face". Most of the time, it probably grazed peacefully on plants. If threatened, Pentaceratops could have charged and jabbed enemies with its spear-like horns. It was three times the weight of today's rhinoceros.

In olden times, soldiers often carried huge clubs to war. **Euoplocephalus** (yoo-oh-plo-sef-al-us) had a club, too – on its tail. This dinosaur's tail ended in two heavy lumps of bone. When in danger, it may have turned around and swiped at its attacker with its tail.

DID DINOSAURS USE WEAPONS?

Swift and silent, **Deinonychus** (dy-non-i-kus) may have raced up behind its prey. Leaping into the air, it probably kicked out with its feet and slashed at the prey with the long, curved claw on the second toe of each foot. When Deinonychus ran, it held these claws clear of the ground to keep them sharp.

Even if you had a dagger, would you attack a powerful creature such as an elephant? Probably not. **Allosaurus** (al-oh-saw-rus) might also have been wary of using its teeth and claws against the mighty bulk of **Diplodocus** (dip-lod-oh-kus). This dinosaur was three times heavier than an elephant! It would probably have lashed with its tail, jabbed with its thumb-spikes, and used its weight to crush Allosaurus.

In a modern army, the tanks and armored cars are well defended. So was the dinosaur **Edmontonia** (ed-mon-toh-nee-ah). It had spikes and shields on its back, longer spikes on its shoulders and sides, and thick plates of bone, like armor-plating. The only place that a predator might have hurt was its soft underbelly.

23

DID DINOSAURS...
Run quickly?

Have you seen a reptile, such as a small lizard, which is warm from sunbathing? It can run so fast that it seems to disappear in a flash. Dinosaurs were reptiles, so they could probably run fast, too. To do this, their bodies would have to be warm from the heat of the sun. When a reptile gets cold it moves more slowly. The fastest dinosaurs had long, slim back legs – the same design as the very speedy bird, the ostrich. A dinosaur with short, thick legs probably lumbered along slowly.

Coelophysis (seel-oh-fy-sis) was one of the thinnest and slimmest of the dinosaurs. It was about 10 feet (3 meters) long and about 3 feet (one meter) high, yet it weighed only 55 pounds (25 kilograms). By flicking its head and neck one way, and its tail the other way, it could probably turn around instantly to chase its prey.

Struthiomimus (stroo-thee-oh-my-mus) was named after the ostrich of today. The name means "ostrich mimic" since it was almost exactly the same size and shape as an ostrich. So Struthiomimus may have been able to run as fast as an ostrich, which is up to 50 miles (80 kilometers) per hour.

DID DINOSAURS RUN QUICKLY?

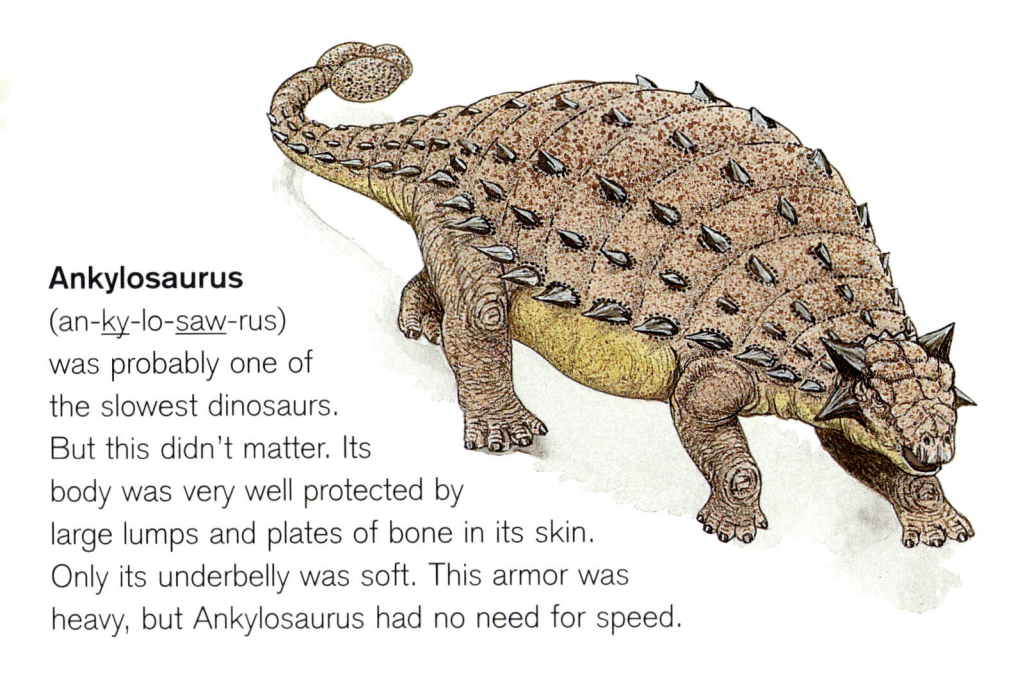

Ankylosaurus
(an-ky-lo-saw-rus) was probably one of the slowest dinosaurs. But this didn't matter. Its body was very well protected by large lumps and plates of bone in its skin. Only its underbelly was soft. This armor was heavy, but Ankylosaurus had no need for speed.

Brachiosaurus
(brak-ee-oh-saw-rus) was so heavy that it could not race along as horses do. It probably plodded like an elephant. Its legs were wide and strong, just like an elephant's legs, but much larger! Brachiosaurus was one of the biggest dinosaurs ever. It was over 80 feet (25 meters) long and stood up to 60 feet (18 meters) tall on its long front legs. It weighed over 65 tons (60 tonnes) – as much as two huge trucks.

Ceratosaurus
(ser-a-toh-saw-rus) had the body shape of a fast-running dinosaur. It had a slim head, a long body, short front legs, very long, strong back legs, and a long tail for balance. Ceratosaurus weighed as much as a hippopotamus, but it could probably run much faster than a hippo.

DID DINOSAURS...
Go swimming?

Some dinosaurs probably went into the water to escape from enemies or to chase prey. They paddled, splashed, and may have swum. But no dinosaurs lived in the water all the time. Three of the creatures shown here, which spent their lives in water, lived at the same time as the dinosaurs. They were reptiles, like the dinosaurs. But they were not dinosaurs. They belonged to other groups of reptiles, which swam in ancient seas.

Plesiosaurs (plez-ee-oh-sors) were fat-bodied reptiles with long necks and short tails. They probably used their paddle-shaped legs to row through the water. There were many kinds of plesiosaur. The biggest grew to be 50 feet (15 meters) long. They fed mainly on fish and sea creatures. Some people believe that a mysterious monster lives in a lake called Loch Ness, in Scotland – and that it's a plesiosaur.

Mosasaurs (mo-za-sors) had huge mouths containing rows of sharp teeth. They were fast swimmers and hunted fish, squid, and curly-shelled ammonites. Ammonites, which were related to squid, have all died out. The biggest mosasaurs were 40 feet (12 meters) long. They were sea lizards, relatives of today's monitor lizards.

DID DINOSAURS GO SWIMMING?

Ichthyosaurs (ik-thee-oh-sors) looked like dolphins, but they were reptiles not mammals. The shape of both dolphins and ichthyosaurs is ideally suited to fast swimming. An ichthyosaur moved by swishing its tail from side to side, and steered with its paddle-shaped legs. It probably fed mainly on fish. Like all the sea reptiles shown here, it had to come to the surface to breathe.

Megalosaurus (meg-a-lo-saw-rus) was a big meat-eating dinosaur. Like most wild animals today, dinosaurs could probably swim when they had to. But they did not spend a long time in the water, especially sea water. The salt in sea water could damage their scales and skin.

Cetiosaurus (see-tee-oh-saw-rus) may have paddled along the beach, but it would not have swum in the ocean unless its life was in danger. Some dinosaurs may have hunted along the beach, but it's unlikely they went into the water. Today, reptiles such as sea snakes and certain types of turtles live in the oceans.

DID DINOSAURS...
Have wings?

No. There were no flying dinosaurs. But there were other flying creatures that lived at the same time. These included dragonflies, and other insects, and the pterosaurs (ter-oh-sors) or "winged reptiles". Pterosaurs looked very much like dinosaurs with wings, but they weren't dinosaurs. They belonged to a different group of reptiles. Also, the first birds appeared during the Age of Dinosaurs. So the skies were probably quite crowded.

Dimorphodon (dy-morf-oh-don) was a pterosaur. It had a large beak-like mouth, and it probably flew over the waves and grabbed fish from just below the water's surface. Its wings measured over 4 feet (1.4 meters) from one tip to the other. Its long tail helped to balance and steer it in flight.

Archaeopteryx (ar-kee-op-ter-ix) was the first bird, as far as we know from fossils. Its fossil bones, beak, and feathers have been found preserved in great detail. Its skeleton is very similar to that of a small dinosaur. But feathers are the key. Any animal with feathers is a bird.

Compsognathus (komp-sog-nay-thus) was one of the smallest dinosaurs. But its tail was actually as long as the rest of its body. It was slim and light, and it could run very fast. It is possible that some kinds of dinosaurs like Compsognathus slowly changed over time into the first birds.

DID DINOSAURS HAVE WINGS?

Quetzalcoatlus (kwet-zal-koht-lus) was the biggest pterosaur and probably glided on the mountain winds. With wings measuring 40 feet (12 meters) across, it was the size of a small aircraft! Yet its body was very light, because many of its bones were tube-like and filled with air. Most pterosaurs had light bones like these.

Pterodaustro (ter-oh-dow-stro) had a long beak-like mouth. The top jaw had a few teeth in it, but the lower jaw had lots of springy bristles instead. This pterosaur may have stood in shallow water and swished its mouth back and forth in the water. It could then swallow any small creatures trapped in the bristles. The great whales of today, like blue whales, feed this way.

Avimimus (av-i-my-mus) is a puzzling dinosaur. Some experts say that tiny marks on its fossil bones show where its feathers were attached. If so, Avimimus might have been a bird, not a dinosaur. The general shape of its skeleton was also very similar to the skeleton of a bird.

WHY DID DINOSAURS...
Die out?

The first dinosaurs appeared on Earth about 230 million years ago. The last dinosaurs lived about 65 million years ago. Then they all died out completely, or became extinct. Dinosaurs weren't the only creatures to disappear at this time. Pterosaurs, sea reptiles and many other kinds of creatures did the same. Some types of plants also became extinct. But the reason these mass deaths happened is still a mystery.

Triceratops (try-serra-tops) lived at the end of the Age of Dinosaurs, 65 million years ago. The sudden disappearance of many kinds of animals and plants is called a mass extinction. This has happened many times during the life of the Earth. In the case of the dinosaurs, was a change to a much colder climate to blame?

Albertosaurus (al-ber-toh-saw-rus), a large dinosaur over 25 feet (about 8 meters) long, was similar to Tyrannosaurus rex. It was one of the last dinosaur survivors. Did these great reptiles die out because of disease? Was shortage of food the cause? Or were they made ill by harmful rays from outer space? Perhaps we will never know.

WHY DID DINOSAURS DIE OUT?

One of the most likely causes of the extinction of the dinosaurs was a huge meteorite from space. A giant lump of rock, perhaps 6 miles (10 kilometers) across, could have smashed into the Earth at incredible speed, making a massive crater. The tremendous explosion would have thrown up clouds of dust and ash. The dust would have blown around the world and blotted out the sun. Without sunlight, plants cannot grow. Without the sun's heat, animals become too cold and die. Is this the real reason dinosaurs no longer exist?

Will dinosaurs ever return?

Not naturally. Thousands of kinds of plants and animals have appeared on Earth, lived for a time, and then gradually died out. It's part of nature. But no plant or animal has ever come back again after becoming extinct. However, modern science could change this. Scientists are testing ways of collecting genes from fossils and other remains of extinct creatures. Genes contain the information on how a living thing is put together. In the far future, perhaps dinosaurs will live again!

Index

Albertosaurus, 30
Allosaurus, 23
Ankylosaurus, 25
Archaeopteryx, 28
Avimimus, 29
Baryonyx, 17
Brachiosaurus, 25
Camarasaurus, 7
Carnotaurus, 19
Ceratosaurus, 25
Cetiosaurus, 27
Chasmosaurus, 12
Coelophysis, 24
Compsognathus, 28
Corythosaurus, 13
Deinonychus, 23

Dilophosaurus, 17
Dimorphodon, 28
Diplodocus, 23
Dromiceiomimus, 6
Edmontonia, 23
Edmontosaurus, 13
Euoplocephalus, 22
Gallimimus, 14
Herrerasaurus, 7
Heterodontosaurus, 6
Ichthyosaurs, 27
Iguanodon, 11
Indosuchus, 10
Kritosaurus, 15
Lesothosaurus, 10
Maiasaura, 8

Mamenchisaurus, 15
Megalosaurus, 27
Microceratops, 21
Mosasaurs, 26
Ornitholestes, 11
Oviraptor, 9
Pachycephalosaurus, 13
Parasaurolophus, 12
Pentaceratops, 22
Plateosaurus, 14
Plesiosaurs, 26
Protoceratops, 8
Psittacosaurus, 13
Pterodaustro, 29
Quetzalcoatlus, 29
Riojasaurus, 7

Saltasaurus, 18
Saltopus, 20
Seismosaurus, 20
Spinosaurus, 19
Stegosaurus, 18
Struthiomimus, 24
Stygimoloch, 19
Styracosaurus, 9
Tarbosaurus, 17
Torosaurus, 21
Triceratops, 30
Tyrannosaurus rex, 21
Velociraptor, 16